Grains with gluten are commonly used to make:

BREAD

BAGELS

DISCARD

PANCAKES AND WAFFLES

FLOUR TORTILLAS

PASTA

MUFFINS

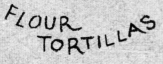

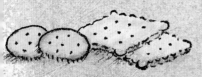

CRACKERS AND BISCUITS

PIZZA

COOKIES

DOUGHNUTS

CUPCAKES

CAKES AND PASTRIES

PIE CRUSTS

For Franny, Elise, Cas, Charlotte, and
all the children battling the crumbs
to live happy, healthy lives —A. R.

For kids everywhere who become
superheroes as they face
their personal challenges! —M. R.

Abigail Rayner grew up mostly in England with a couple of years in Greece thrown in.
She moved to New York City in her twenties, where she worked as a reporter for British
newspapers. Her books, *The Backup Bunny* (2018) and *I Am a Thief* (2019) called
"Hilarious and sweet" by *Kirkus Reviews* (starred review), have delighted children.
This is her third picture book for NorthSouth Books. She lives in New Jersey, with her
husband, two kids, two cats, and lots of tasty gluten-free snacks.

Molly Ruttan is from Hastings-on-Hudson, New York, where she and her twin sister
grew up drawing and creating plush toys, board games, and, of course, books! Molly
attended Cooper Union School of Art in New York City. She graduated with a BFA in
graphic design. Her first picture book for NorthSouth, *I Am a Thief* (2019) called
"Hilarious and sweet" by *Kirkus Reviews* (starred review), is a delight. She is married
to Gabriel Moffat, her childhood sweetheart and a fellow musician. They have three
daughters, three dogs, one cat, one brand-new grandchild and at least one cupboard
full of gluten-free goodies.

Abigail Rayner  Molly Ruttan

Violet
and the
Crumbs
A Gluten-Free Adventure

North
South

Violet used to love birthday parties,
but things have changed.
Now she's not allowed to eat pizza or cake
because of the gluten—it's even in the crumbs.

Violet has celiac disease.
It means her body does not like gluten.
That's the stretchy stuff in dough.
The dough that makes bread, pizza,
and cake …

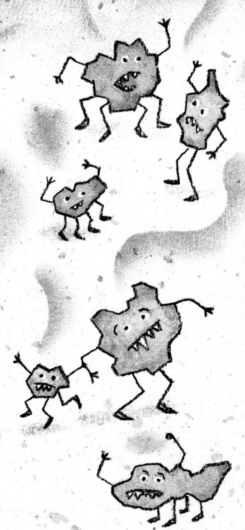

and **CRUMBS**.

The cells in Violet's
body turn into soldiers
when they see gluten.
They try to fight it.

But they give Violet
a tummy ache instead.
Just one teeny crumb
of gluten can make
her sick.

Violet says, "Please can you use a fork?
Otherwise gluten crumbs might get
on the fruit."

But her voice is too quiet.

She hates to seem like a fusspot.

Sometimes people try to be kind. "We made a gluten-free cake so you could have it too!" That's the worst thing of all.

A gluten-free cake has to be prepared and baked in a place that has no gluten crumbs, otherwise it is not gluten-free.

Violet has to say "No thank you."

Violet stops going to parties.

She takes some desperate measures
to defy the crumbs at school.

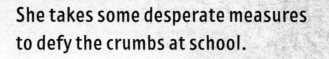

Now Violet feels safe!

But she
is lonely.

She can't be
the only one ...

... can she?

ANIMAL DIETS

FEED HAY
& PELLETS
NO BREAD
COOKIES OR
CRACKERS

NACHO

Violet discovers that food that contains gluten can be bad for some animals too!

VIOLET TO THE RESCUE!

"Stop!"

Bread is not healthy for ducks.
"Feed them cracked corn
or cooked rice."

"Wait!"

Hedgehogs can't eat bread!
"Give them cat food and plain
old water."

Bread is harmful
to squirrels too.

"Hey, Merv!
Drop the bagel!"

It's nice to know she's not the only one with dietary restrictions.

But it doesn't make school any easier.

Violet is tired
of missing out on
all the fun.

She is sick of
being alone!

BACK-TO-SCHOOL
HARVEST
FESTIVAL
POTLUCK

It feels like celiac
has taken a big bite
out of her life.

Plus, her suit is hot.

Violet gets an idea. She has spoken up for the hedgehogs, the ducks, and the squirrels. Now she needs to stand up for herself.

BACK TO SCHOOL
HARVEST FESTIVAL

The idea makes her chest tight, but Violet decides to be brave.

The children ask lots of questions.
Violet tells them about the
evil gluten crumbs, and it turns out ...

they don't think Violet
is a fusspot at all!

NOT
G.F.
←

After that things get a lot easier.

Crumbs don't even seem evil anymore!

At Halloween Violet has fun trading candy.

She hosts gluten-free baking classes at her house.

And when it's time to celebrate Violet's birthday,
there isn't a single crumb in sight.

Even better ...

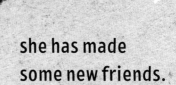

she has made
some new friends.

About Celiac Disease

Celiac disease is an autoimmune disease that runs in families. When a person with celiac disease eats gluten, the body sees it as an enemy, and the immune system attacks.

Gluten is a protein found in wheat, barley, and rye. People with celiac disease must avoid foods that contain wheat, barley, and rye, such as bread, pizza, and birthday cake.

Even a tiny crumb can make a person with celiac disease sick. This is why Violet can't eat the watermelon that another child has touched—in case any gluten crumbs have stuck to the watermelon. When food such as pizza or bread comes into contact with gluten-free food, via fingers, utensils, baking pans, or chopping boards, it is no longer safe for a person with celiac disease to eat. This is called cross-contact. When people with celiac disease eat gluten, the body mounts an immune response that attacks the small intestine. The small intestine is where food goes after it has been in the stomach and before it gets to the large intestine. The small intestine is lined with villi that look like tiny fingers and whose job it is to absorb nutrients. When people with celiac disease eat gluten, the villi become damaged. For this reason people with undiagnosed celiac disease don't get all the nutrients they need. Celiac disease affects one in a hundred people, but 80 percent don't even know they have it.

Most people, even some doctors, don't know much about celiac disease. You can help spread the word by talking about it, or reading this book, to people you know. The only treatment for celiac disease is a strict gluten-free diet. There is currently no cure, but as long as people with celiac disease follow a strict gluten-free diet, most live long, healthy lives.

Grains, starches, or flours that can be part of a **gluten-free diet** include:

 AMARANTH

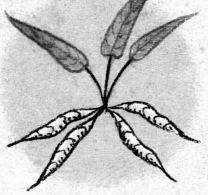 ARROWROOT

 BUCKWHEA

 FLAX

 MILLET

 OATS **

SORGHUM

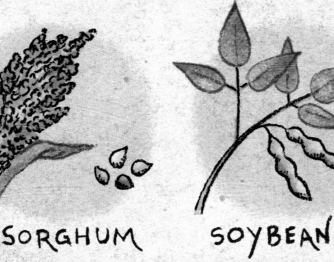 SOYBEAN

TEFF